Love & Lattes

A sweet romance short story collection

JESSICA EISSFELDT

Love & Lattes: A sweet romance short story
collection
Jessica Eissfeldt

ISBN: 978-1-989290-15-6

ALSO BY JESSICA EISSFELDT

Sweet Historical Romance

Sweethearts & Jazz Nights
Dialing Dreams
Shattered Melodies
Fancy Footwork
Unspoken Lyrics
The Sweethearts & Jazz Nights Boxed Set: The Complete Collection

Love By Moonlight
Beneath A Venetian Moon
Besides A Moonlit Shore
The Love By Moonlight Boxed Set: The Complete Collection

Sweet Contemporary Romance

Prince Edward Island Love Letters & Legends
This Time It's Forever
Now It's For Always
At Last It's True Love

Collections

Love & Lattes: A Sweet Romance Short Story Collection

Chick Lit

Love, Your Fangirl

Dear reader:

I combed through my writing files one day and came across this series of short stories that I'd nearly forgotten I'd written. I penned them in the early days of my novelist career, originally having written and submitted six of these seven stories to *Woman's World* magazine. When the first six of these short sweet romances didn't end up being published by *Woman's World*, I decided I'd like to publish them anyway for you to enjoy. The seventh story, *Heading Toward Hopeful*, had originally appeared in a literary magazine.

Happy reading!

Jessica Eissfeldt
August 2018

Snapshot of Love

SARA SMILED AS she took a breath of the refreshing spring breeze and tilted her face to the sunshine. A perfect day for some snapshots. She entered the wrought iron gates of the public park, her Nikon around her neck.

On a day as beautiful as this, she wasn't going to sit on the sidelines any longer. Even though Dave had broken up with her last month.

Her sneakers crunched on the winding gravel path as she passed joggers, moms with strollers, and people feeding pigeons.

She began snapping, making her way to the pond in the middle of the park, surrounded by willow and oak trees.

The sunlight sparkled on the water at just the right angle, and the swaying branches of the willow trees almost concealed the wooden park benches set underneath their spreading roots.

She kept walking, eye to her viewfind-

er, finger on the shutter. These would make great prints.

"Excuse me?" said a male voice behind her.

"Oh!" she said, glancing up from her viewfinder. A man sat on the park bench, a Canon DSLR in his hands. She felt a warm flush spread onto her cheeks. "I didn't see you there."

"Didn't mean to scare you." He smiled, but his expression changed to confusion as he held up the Canon. "I was just trying to figure this thing out and thought you might be able to help. There are so many settings and buttons and dials...." He trailed off, running a hand through his hair, then looking back up at her, his blue eyes sincere. "It's a bit overwhelming to a beginning shutterbug like me."

Sara tucked her own camera into her purse. Wanting to help him, she took a seat on the next bench over. She couldn't help but admire the way his dark hair fell appealingly into his eyes.

"What do you need help with?"

He fumbled with the heavy camera, tilting it up with one hand while scratching his head with the other. "Like I said, I'm a newbie. I love photography, though." He flashed a grin.

Even though they'd only been chatting for a minute, Sara felt herself relax in his company. "I've been doing photography for about four years now and I love it, too. But I remember when I first started, I felt really intimidated by all the dials and gadgets on my camera, too. In fact, I always had it on the auto setting." She laughed. "So I can understand."

He looked at her. "I'm Todd, by the way." He extended a hand, then chuckled self-consciously. She stood up from her bench and walked over to shake his hand.

"I'm Sara." As their hands clasped, she felt the warmth of his palm against hers. Her heart fluttered as she took a chance and decided to sit down next to him instead of returning to her own bench. She couldn't help noticing his spicy cologne. "So, what's the problem?"

"It's this setting here." He pointed to the camera's digital screen. "I can't get it to turn the flash off. It's stuck on or something." He frowned again.

"Oh," Sara said, "that's an easy fix. It's just this button here... You actually have to press down and then flick this switch." She demonstrated with her own camera.

She watched Todd as he followed her instructions. Sara smiled to herself and a glow of satisfaction spread through her when she saw his smile of triumph emerge.

"Thanks so much," Todd said, looking up from the camera's screen. "If you hadn't shown me what to do, I probably would've been sitting here for hours flipping through the manual." He laughed, a sparkle in his eye. "Guys do read directions from time to time, you know. If they're desperate. But it's a trade secret. Don't tell anyone."

"Girl scout's honor." She raised her right hand and joined in with his laughter as the warm sunshine soaked into her. The green leaves of the weeping willow waved gently in the breeze.

"Oh no!" Sara said. "What time is it?"

"Just after 1 p.m.," Todd said.

"After 1?" She jumped up from the bench. "I have to go or I'll miss my bus – my sister's expecting me to babysit her kids this afternoon." She hurried on, "It was nice meeting you, and good luck with your photography."

He looked up. "Thanks! You too."

She turned and hurried down the path toward the park entrance, and caught sight of the bus as it pulled across the intersection just before her stop. She quickened her pace. Would she ever make a lasting connection with someone new? She broke into a sprint as she saw her bus pull up to the stop by the gate.

"Wait! Sara!"

She glanced over her shoulder. It was Todd, jogging after her. "You forgot your camera."

"Oh – thank you." She slowed and he caught up to her.

"I know you're in a hurry, but do you want to take some snapshots with me, down on the waterfront this evening around 7, after you're done babysitting?" He handed her the Nikon.

"I'd like that." She grinned as she boarded the bus. "See you then!"

Ingredients For Love

AS HE DASHED from the warm, dry interior of the taxi to the cold, wet curb, Ben hugged the paper grocery bags tightly. He hunched his broad shoulders against the pouring rain as he darted across the street. Only a few more steps and he'd be there. A flash of bright red caught his eye, and he glanced up to see a young woman unlocking the door of a nearby townhouse, red umbrella in hand.

But with the ingredients for a birthday cake piled high in the grocery bags, Ben didn't see the large puddle before he splashed into it. He slipped, and sent the bags flying out of his arms.

Luckily, he regained his balance. The eggs, however, weren't so lucky. They landed with a splat on the damp sidewalk. Right beside the fallen and now-soaked bags of flour and sugar.

Ben sighed in frustration and checked his watch. No time to go back to the store before his nephew's surprise birthday party. What could he do? He began gathering up the spilled contents.

Just then, the young woman carrying the red umbrella approached.

"You okay?" she asked.

He nodded, and his heart sped up as he glanced at her. She looked familiar.

He took a second glance. Yes. There was no mistaking the curly brown hair and the heart-shaped face. "Danielle Fulham?" He cleared his throat and stood. "I haven't seen you since...senior year of high school. You went to Ridgemont, right?"

She nodded. "Small world, huh? And you're Ben Moore."

"Small city, at least." He smiled at her.

"I just moved to town, actually." She gestured to the spilled contents of the bags. "Can I help?"

"I don't want to bother you, but I have a birthday cake to make for my nephew's surprise party and don't have enough time to go back to the store. I don't suppose you have a spare carton of eggs handy? My eggs have scrambled on the sidewalk." He grinned wryly.

She smiled back. "Let me go check. I

live right here." She pointed to the townhouse nearby. Ben watched her duck inside. That was generous of her. How could he make it up to her? Maybe lunch? But was she single?

She returned a few minutes later, carton of eggs in hand. "Here you go." She flashed him that smile of hers. Something he couldn't forget. And no wedding ring, either, he noticed as he took the cardboard container from her grasp.

"Are you sure? This is more than generous. I can pay you back for it. I have some cash here." He fumbled with his jacket, and started to pull out his wallet.

But she waved it away. "I get this stuff on discount. I manage an organic grocery chain now. Just enjoy your nephew's party."

He glanced at his watch and realized he was now even later. "I'm really sorry but I have to run. Probably literally." He laughed and she chimed in.

"Watch out for those puddles," she called.

"I will. It was good to see you again, Danielle." He waved, then turned the corner to go into his place.

After his nephew's party, Ben found his thoughts straying to Danielle again. It had been awhile since he'd dated anyone. And she'd always been kind, he remembered, even in high school, even to a klutzy guy like him with a secret crush on her.

Could it really have been that long ago that he'd been too shy to ask her to the school dance? Or even out on a regular date? She'd always had boyfriends, anyway. But working together on a science fair project had been the highlight of his senior year, maybe even his whole high school career, he thought.

He had to do something. He couldn't let this opportunity slip through his fingers again. After he pulled on a raincoat, he grabbed the dozen replacement eggs he'd bought, tucked them under his arm and headed back down to her townhouse.

He knocked on her door and shifted his weight from foot to foot, wondering if she'd be there. Wondering if she'd even be interested in him after all this time.

He hit the buzzer again, his hopes falling. He must have just missed her. But as he turned to go, the sound Ben the door opening stopped him. Turning around, he

looked into her warm brown eyes.

He held out the eggs. "The look on my nephew's face was priceless when he saw that cake. Thank you."

She wound a curl around her finger. "I'm glad."

"Um, there's one other thing that I, uh, wanted to ask."

"Oh? What's that?"

"Can I make you some lunch?"

"That sounds great," she said.

He grinned. "I have all the ingredients."

Art of the Heart

FAWN'S EYES WIDENED as she wiped away layers of dust. The painting's brushstrokes revealed a study of lilies floating on serene waters. Could it really be an undiscovered Monet like the old woman had said?

The shop's bell jarred her and she looked up. A customer? Now? But it was almost closing. On a Friday. She straightened up and looked into a pair of green eyes.

"Mark Henderson. I'm with the art crimes division of the FBI. I need to see your shop license. And your recently acquired art." He flashed his badge.

Fawn bristled. "This shop has been in my family for years. We're a respected and reputable Upper East Side antiques emporium. I – "

Mark held up a hand. "Relax, ma'am. I'm not slapping cuffs on you." He lowered his voice, and tempered it with a smile.

"There's been a rash of art forgeries in the past six months. We're checking all the antique stores in the city."

Fawn breathed a sigh of relief and reached behind the register to pull out the deed. "Will this do?"

The FBI agent nodded. Smiled again. Fawn noticed his dimple. No ring, either. Her heart sped up.

"And your art?" He raised a dark brow at the canvas on the counter.

"I just got this yesterday."

"I'll have to take it in. Run some tests."

Her grip tightened on the cracked frame. She couldn't part with a potential masterpiece until she knew for certain who had painted it. "Don't you need a warrant?"

"Not for this." But Mark's expression was kind. "If it makes you feel better, you can come in too. Make sure I'm not stealing it." His green eyes twinkled.

She couldn't help smiling at his joke. "All right."

As they rode the elevator to the 40th floor of the FBI building, Fawn's mind drifted over the past year's events. Since her divorce, Fawn had poured her energy into her antique shop. She loved every moment of helping customers, and thrilled in finding the occasional rare piece. But she'd never found a treasure like this painting. Until now. She snuck a glance at Mark in his suit and tie. He certainly was handsome. And seemed kind. But Fawn brushed the thoughts away. Running her antique shop was her focus. She didn't have time for romance.

They stepped into a brightly lit conference room. Drawn to the wall of windows, Fawn gazed at the sparkling waters of New York Harbor, the Statue of Liberty tiny yet triumphant on her pedestal.

Mark stepped up to her shoulder. "That view never gets old." They looked out at the summer skyline in companionable silence. "But this trail might get cold if we don't take a look at what you have here."

He indicated a chair.

"What can you remember about the person who brought it in?"

"The old woman had cleaned out her attic and thought it might be valuable; a Monet, according to family stories. Said she had some debts to pay off." Fawn admired the painting's colors, the golden light of evening captured perfectly. If it

was a Monet, she could donate it to the Met. Suddenly, a name came back to her. "She said her family name was Dauphne."

Mark looked up from his notebook and into her eyes. "A name is definitely a place to start. You're free to go, but I'm afraid this painting needs to stay overnight."

Fawn stood.

Mark escorted her down to the lobby. "If you remember anything else, here's my card."

As she took it, their fingers brushed and their eyes met. She smiled shyly. Neither spoke for a heartbeat.

Back in her shop, Fawn debated and paced. Should she have told him she thought it was real? She supposed the crime lab would find out soon enough. No. She shook her head. This was her art, her life, her shop. She had to go back.

She checked her watch. But would he still be there? It was getting late. She retraced her steps back to FBI headquarters; her heart sank when she tried the doors. Locked. She pulled out her phone to dial the number on his card but her phone's screen stayed dark. No battery.

After hailing a cab, she headed back to

her shop. And stopped short on the sidewalk outside the front door when she saw Mark there. He spoke. "I wanted to tell you in person. The painting wasn't a forgery."

Fawn held her breath. "No?"

"But it wasn't a lost master's work, either."

Fawn frowned.

"It was an early contemporary of Monet's, the lab said. And that family name you gave us? Well, those family stories must've gotten a bit mixed up over time—because she's the great-grandniece of the painter himself."

"So you didn't catch your thief?"

He looked into her eyes. "Not yet. But I did find something valuable."

She felt her cheeks flush.

"Do you want to get a latte? Who knows, you might discover a Renoir behind the till." He winked.

She laughed. Maybe a bit of romance was just what she needed. "I'm up for that adventure."

On Butterfly Wings

*L*ESLEY BLINKED ONCE, twice, then cocked her head in surprise and looked closer. No, she wasn't mistaken. It was the exact same type of blue butterfly that had been outlined in gold on her grandmother's favorite tea set. She watched it flap its wings, then lift off from the pink rosebud.

Her grandmother's words flitted through Lesley's mind as she watched the dainty insect fly away. *My dear, the heart always finds a way.*

Lesley's grandmother had always been there to give Lesley advice and support. But after her grandmother passed away last spring, Lesley felt lost. Until the butterflies started appearing.

She began noticing that whenever she thought of her grandmother, she almost always saw a butterfly that same day. On a T-shirt. Or a billboard. Or even, one time, on a teenager's backpack.

But this was the first time she'd seen an actual blue butterfly. Good thing she'd decided to take a trip to the local butterfly garden on her lunch break.

"Beautiful, aren't they?" said a male voice behind her.

Lesley, caught off-guard, turned toward the voice. It came from a handsome man in a casual pair of jeans and green staff T-shirt.

"Yes, amazing. This is my first time to the gardens, actually."

"Then you're in for a treat." His gaze fell warmly on hers.

Lesley couldn't help but return his friendly smile.

"Have you been a butterfly enthusiast long?"

Lesley blushed. How could she begin to tell him she'd simply stepped into the place on a whim that had nothing to do with science and everything to do with her bond with her grandmother?

"Oh, I, well...I'm just..." She trailed off.

"My first time in here left me a little speechless, too," he said.

They stood in companionable silence for a few moments, just watching the

kaleidoscope of color around them.

Lesley unzipped her purse and looked at her phone just as a pair of butterflies flew by. "I'd better head back to the office. My lunch break's almost over. But it was nice talking with you, uh,—"

"Luke." He extended his hand. She clasped it, and his warm fingers gently closed around hers.

"I'm Lesley."

A round of urgent buzzing had Luke pulling out his phone. "That's my boss. I hope you enjoy the rest of the gardens," he said before he headed off.

Lesley wished she had had more time to chat with Luke, as she walked to the exit and out into the bright sunshine.

Back at the office, Lesley tried to settle into her afternoon routine but found herself remembering Luke instead. She sighed. She hadn't been on a date in over six months. But if he'd been interested, she supposed he would've asked her on the spot. Wouldn't he?

The end of the day arrived with him still on her mind. Reaching into her purse for her car keys, she frowned, then double-checked her purse and her pockets. Her keys were missing. Maybe they'd fallen out at the gardens? She had unzipped her purse there, after all.

She called a cab and headed over to the butterfly garden grounds. The driver pulled into the almost-empty lot. "Can you wait, please?" Lesley asked. "I just need to check if my keys are here."

Lesley walked past the gate and the office, and into the gardens. She retraced her steps around the winding pathways, finding neither her keys nor any staff members. Well, someone had to be here. There had been a car in the lot.

She nudged aside the disappointment at not seeing Luke. There was just one spot left to check.

Lesley headed back to the fountain she and Luke had been standing beside earlier that day.

She scanned the ground. Nothing. Had someone stolen them?

Her heart plummeted and she frowned. Now what?

Well, maybe she hadn't lost them here. She started back the way she came. As she rounded the curve in the walkway, she heard someone approach. She looked up and her heart jumped. It was the same man from that afternoon. Luke.

He held out her keys.

"I had a feeling these might be yours when I picked them up by the fountain, but you'd already left." He handed the keyring to her and continued. "I didn't know how to get ahold of you, so I'd set them aside for the lost and found. Then when I was in the office just now, I saw you come in, but couldn't find you 'til I came out here. These paths can be kind of like a maze. I'm glad you made it back here." He grinned.

"Oh, thank you so much!" Lesley sighed in relief as she took the keyring from Luke. "When I got here and couldn't find them, I thought maybe I was too late."

"Just in time," he assured her, as he met her gaze. "There is one thing I'd like to know, though."

She felt her cheeks grow warm. "What's that?"

"Would you like to go on a nature walk with me?"

Just then, Lesley noticed a blue butter-fly swoop in front of them.

The heart always does find a way, Lesley thought. Nodding to Luke, she simply said, "Yes."

A Chemistry Lesson

C HLOE WHEELED THE shelving cart into the non-fiction section of the Goodwell Library and smiled. Her job never got old.

So much knowledge here. So many books. And, she'd discovered, no matter what library she visited, she could always count on feeling at home.

She pulled the cart to a stop at the end of the aisle of science books and picked up the heavy chemistry textbook.

She scooted between the bookshelf and the study table at the end of the row, occupied by a handsome brown-haired man surrounded by piles of books open on the table around him.

He glanced up at her as he moved his chair out of her way, and their eyes met. "Thanks," she said.

"You're welcome," he replied.

She noticed the calculator, graph paper and notebook. A grad student? Hmm. Or

maybe a teacher?

Carefully, she maneuvered the heavy textbook up to the very top shelf, trying to balance it with one hand while she shifted the other books over to make room with the other. Not a wise move.

The heavy science book wobbled, and before she could stop it, it fell from her grasp.

"Watch out!" she exclaimed to the man at the table. But it was too late. The book fell, just missing his head and her toes, before it landed, facedown, on the floor.

"You okay?" He got to his feet, looking at Chloe.

She nodded. "I'm sorry. Those books can be heavy."

"Here." He stooped down and picked up the chemistry textbook with one hand. "These have a way of jumping out at you." He stood up and put the book on the high shelf for her.

"Thanks."

"I'm Nate, by the way."

"Chloe." She smiled as she looked into his green eyes. "You knew exactly where that went."

He sat again, and indicated the piles of

books around him. "I spend quite a bit of time in libraries. I tutor when I'm not teaching. This year I didn't have a full course load to prep for, so I decided to do some volunteering. Have you worked at the library long?"

"I started a few years ago. I love books."

"Me too. All that knowledge at your fingertips."

"Exactly," she said. Then she paused. "Well, I guess I'd better keep shelving here. Nice talking with you, though."

"Same here. Maybe I'll see you around another night."

She smiled as she walked away, and the rest of her shift flew by. Would he be there again tomorrow?

But he wasn't. Nor the next night.

She tried to forget about him but she couldn't. Had he decided to go to a different library? But then, the following night, he appeared again. This time with a student.

He smiled at her as she shelved the physics and astronomy books near his table and she smiled back before continuing on her rounds.

The lights flicked once. Twice. The ten-minute warning. She headed back to his table, and saw that the student had gone.

"Nate, we're closing in ten minutes."

He looked up. "Thanks for letting me know, Chloe."

"You know," she said, "I had to take remedial chemistry. But it seems like you have a knack for explaining difficult concepts."

"That's what I love about the libraries – they help people understand things. That's also what I love about my work. It's so rewarding to see the light of understanding dawn on a student's face. Just like that old cliché – 'knowledge is power.'"

Chloe nodded. "I feel that way about books. Helping patrons find just the right book. There's something almost magical about it." She blushed. Had she revealed too much about herself?

But the light of understanding that lit his green eyes to a soft glowing emerald had her sighing in relief.

On impulse, she moved closer. "I know the library's closing now, but there's a lecture tonight at the community college on the history of libraries. Do you want to go with me?" She waited, holding her breath.

He looked at his notebook, then back up at her. "That sounds great."

Turtle Tracks

ABBY GLANCED OUT the car window at the coastline and grinned as a tingle of excitement ran through her. Finally in San Diego. Even though the city was only an hour from Abby's home, she hadn't found the time to drive down to the sea turtle research center that she'd always wanted to visit. Being a single mom, all her time and attention, when she wasn't working at the vet hospital, was for her two-year-old, Gabriella. And so Abby's own dream of helping sea turtles had taken a back seat to raising her daughter.

But now that Abby's sister had moved into town and volunteered to babysit Gabriella on Saturdays, Abby had finally been convinced it was safe to take a day off and go pursue one of her dreams.

Abby watched the waves wash the shoreline as she pulled the car into the parking lot. After she slipped off her sunglasses, she stepped out of the car. She spotted a group of people on the beach in front of the parking lot, and headed over to them.

"Excuse me. Do you know where I sign in? I'm volunteering for the day."

They directed her to the back door of the single-story brick building.

Abby walked back up the path toward the center and noticed a tanned blond man wearing a white T-shirt and khaki shorts standing in the doorway. Another volunteer? Or maybe one of the researchers? Her heart sped up for a second at his good looks.

He greeted her with an open smile and friendly hazel eyes. "I'm Matt, the facility coordinator. You must be our help for today."

Abby smiled back and shook his hand. "Abby."

"I'll give you a tour of the place and then show you what you're going to be doing for the day."

"Sounds great."

As they walked into the building, Abby found herself confiding, "You know, I've always wanted to do this."

"It's definitely a great feeling to help

those that can't help themselves," he said.

"Exactly." Abby glanced at him out of the corner of her eye and smoothed down her ponytail.

"And this is where we set things up for the volunteers." Matt held open an inner door for her and she looked around at the equipment. "You really love your job, don't you?" she said softly.

"Yes."

Abby saw the pride and compassion in his eyes as he continued, telling her about habitat restructuring and nesting numbers; it tugged at her heart. He turned to her. "Did you know all seven of the world's sea turtle species are endangered?"

Abby shook her head, then smiled. The way Matt spoke about aquatic animals with such passion and conviction sent goose bumps up her arms.

Matt led her outside and along the sand to a staked-off area. "This is your nest to monitor for today."

Abby took the clipboard he handed her and listened as he told her what to check for and how to make note of any changes.

"We're expecting the hatchlings any day now," Matt explained.

"That's so exciting!" Abby looked down at the nest. "This reminds me of pulling an all-night shift at the vet hospital when we get stray dogs with litters of puppies."

"It's a bit like that, yes." Matt held her gaze a moment longer, the warmth of understanding passing between them before he turned back to the facility.

While Abby filled out the paperwork on the clipboard, she couldn't help but remember the expression on Matt's face as he'd regarded her.

Could she hope for romance after all this time alone? She shook her head. She was here to live a dream, not pick up a man. Besides, she didn't know if he liked kids. Or if he was even single.

Abby returned to the facility's office after making the necessary notes. She was just about to leave the clipboard at the unmanned desk when Matt came around the corner. She handed the clipboard to him.

"Very professional." He glanced at the notes and then up at her. "Usually volun-teers aren't nearly so thorough as all this."

"Like I said, it pays to work at a vet

hospital." She grinned.

He grinned back. "It's refreshing. Especially since this information is so important for our research." He paused, then added, "You know, sea turtle habitat shrinks more and more each year. Even more so around here."

Abby shook her head. "That's so sad. Environmental awareness is vital – especially for kids. Well, speaking for myself and my own daughter."

Matt nodded. "That's why giving the kids' tour is my favorite part of the job."

"Oh, really?" Abby felt a happy thrill.

Matt said, "You know, it seems we have a lot in common. Want to grab a smoothie?"

"I'd like that," Abby said. As they headed out the door, Abby smiled. Maybe it was possible to follow her dreams and find love, too.

Heading Toward Hopeful

E LOOKS MORE like a painting than a real man. Like one of those oil works from the early 1800s. His fair skin, dark hair, high cheekbones and brown eyes seem to have been given three-dimensional life by wizardry wafted over a cracked canvas in some aristocrat's attic.

Come on, Gemma, get a grip. This is the 21st century. And you're on a bus. Deep breaths.

But my mind whirls back through the facts. Mystery bus man and I have been exchanging glances for several months now.

This is ridiculous. Totally and utterly insane! Yet I still steal a traitorous glance sideways. Despite the packed bus, he notices. His eyes shift right. Across the narrow aisle, mine shift left. Seconds pass like minutes, neither of us looking away.

Then it happens. Again. I try to fight the pure electricity that jolts through me as the thought *who is he?* runs through my mind. I jerk my head away and stare firmly out the steamy window.

My stop. Too rapidly, I'm vectored forward out of my plastic seat and barely snag one purse strap as the bus doors hydraulic open. I slip on the November puddle in the doorway and nearly fall as I step onto the pavement just past the Old Burying Ground on Spring Garden Road.

The spikes topping the ancient wrought-iron seem to have sprung tears as clinging droplets slide over the fence while the rain patters down through the oak leaves lining the cemetery grounds.

I flinch at the sight and avert my eyes, gripping my yellow umbrella more firmly and heading in the direction of the Metro Guide Publishing office a few blocks away.

The thud, thud, thud of leather shoes echoes behind me. I'm about to dodge out of the way, but a voice sounds in my ear before I can move.

"Excuse me?"

I whirl around, nearly jabbing a tall stranger in the eye with my portable rain-cover. I inhale rain droplets as well as brisk air – bus man speaks. *Oh no.* I stiffen. *He's probably going to hit on me like that weirdo with dreds in the checkout line last week.* I begin shifting my body weight backward.

"Yes?" Reluctantly, I meet his gaze, hoping I don't sound too curt...or too eager... *Okay, so why do I even care?*

"This fell out of your purse." He holds up my cell phone.

"Oh." I hesitantly open my palm, breathe a hasty thank you and spin on my heel, rapidly retreating in case he tries to say anything else.

I FURTIVELY GLANCE at the passengers embarking the next morning as the bus pulls up to Quinpool Road across from the Atlantic Superstore. My pulse speeds and the square of cardboard crumples slightly in my palm when, sure enough, bus man strides on. He walks past me, throwing the smallest hint of a nod in my direction. I smile back, then duck my head.

He sits down behind me and I tense. It's now or never – he's probably not going to be this close to me again.

Maybe I shouldn't be doing this. It's too soon. But he gave me back my phone, I rationalize with myself. *So why not?!*

I twist in my seat and meet his gaze. "Listen, do you want to get a coffee with me this afternoon?" I let out the breath I didn't realize I was holding, a surge of confidence replacing my fear of moments before.

He blinks. I wait, feeling doubt slide in sideways.

"Okay, sure," he replies.

"Great!" I can't help grinning, passing him my card. "At 5:30 at Uncommon Grounds on Barrington?"

"Got it." He pockets my card and hands me his own. "My name's Christian, by the way."

I SHAKE THE water off my umbrella and step into the tiny yet trendy low-ceiled bistro.

We grab drinks and I wrap my hands around the steaming mug of chai latte, inhaling the familiar aroma of cinnamon and nutmeg. "So." I take a sip. "Have you been in Halifax long?"

"Born and raised here."

"Oh yeah? I'm from Saskatchewan. But moved here for a job at Metro Guide Publishing more or less a year ago."

"Ah, so that's why I hadn't seen you on the bus before then." He speaks with open frankness. "So you're a journalist?"

I nod. "And what do you do?"

"I'm an architect over in the Purdy's Wharf II building. Been there a few years now."

"You like designing stuff?"

He grins. "I just love the way old houses, and all architecture, really, have such a grace to them, you know?"

He gestures with a sweeping motion. "It's like the lines you trace on the drafting board...seeing that come to life...there's just something so, well, almost spiritual about it."

His expression holds an expansiveness and ease as he studies me over the rim of his cup, the passion of his words striking a resonance in my soul that I'm not ready to admit. I bite my lower lip, eyes flicking to the tabletop as my hands clench around my drink.

The intensity of his gaze slices into me. I shift back in my seat.

He takes another sip of his coffee, oblivious to my internal struggle. "Seems to me, there's this creative power within, just waiting to be realized. Do you feel that way when you're writing?" He leans in, wanting reciprocity.

There's expectancy in his face. I pull back. The idea of sharing with him suddenly has me gasping for breath. I open my mouth, but no sound comes out. I try again, "I...," I swallow, meeting his gaze, "...I..."

The rough scrape of my chair over the tile floor interrupts any comment he might make.

I throw a few half-babbled sentences at him, not even listening to any questioning protests he tries to utter. All I feel is guilt crashing around me like a savage storm. Flinging my purse over my shoulder, I push my way out of the coffee shop and into the Thursday evening rush.

I don't dare glance anywhere but straight ahead as I brush salty drops from my face, hoping yet not hoping he'll somehow catch up to me. But the whiz of traffic is my only escort as I head back home, defeated.

THE EARLY-MORNING LIGHT gilds the harbor and transitions the pale blue sky a hopeful pink as I pay the cashier and make my way back up the hill. Settling myself onto a faded bench, I slowly pull out my cell phone, dialing the number and smiling as I hear it ring.

"Hello?"

"Hi. Christian? It's Gemma. Listen, I'm really sorry about yesterday. I feel bad and I'd like to make it up to you somehow. Do you have time right now to meet me for a short walk?"

There's a pause. Then, "Sure. Where are you?"

"The Old Burying Ground."

"The cemetery? This morning?"

"Please, just come."

"Okay, I'll be there in ten."

"See you then." I press end and finger the velvety white long-stem beside me on the bench. *Am I doing the right thing? Can I do this?* A memory of the look in his eyes bolsters my courage. *Yes, I can!*

Footfalls reach my ears and I turn to see Christian striding through the

wrought-iron gateway. I stand up, holding the rose and a tray with two coffees.

I proffer a drink. "Some morning java?"

"Thanks." He takes one, the steam curling up into the dawn. "Is that for me?" He raises a brow and nods at the rose in my hand.

I take a deep breath, shaking my head. "No. It's actually not."

"Then...?"

Before he says anything else, I start walking, the sunlight shining a golden path up the slope. Stopping in front of a granite headstone, I sink to my knees, resting the rose's petals against the now-frozen earth. I turn my head, look up at him.

"It's for my fiancé." My voice surprises me with a tone of confidence as I wait for his reaction.

He places a hand gently on my shoulder. "I get it," he murmurs, the sincerity in his tone melting my anxiety. "I get it. My wife died three years ago. Sometimes it helps to talk about it."

A warmth steals through me as I exhale, all my vulnerability exposed. Yet it's as if the fears evaporate in the purity of the morning sun. The beams turn his eyes a caramel-brown and it's in that moment I know I can trust him – and trust myself – again.

"I'm a good listener." He smiles.

This time, I don't run.

Thanks for reading! Want more sweet romance?

Turn the page to find out more!

FOR A LIMITED TIME
GET YOUR FREE SWEET ROMANCE HERE!

Get your free copy of the sweet romance *Beside A Moonlit Shore*. Normally, it's $2.99, but this GIFT is yours FREE when you sign up to hear from author Jessica Eissfeldt.

When you sign up, not only will you get this FREE GIFT, but you'll also receive sneak peaks of Jessica's upcoming stories, have the opportunity to win prizes, get exclusive subscriber-only content...and more!

After her sea captain husband dies, schoolteacher Anna Hampton wonders if she'll find the courage to love again...beside a moonlit shore.

Go here to get started:
www.jessicaeissfeldt.com/yourfreegift

FOR A LIMITED TIME

Acknowledgments

Shannon Page—copyeditor/proof reader, who had a great eye for detail

Angela Waters—cover designer, who gave me a great cover for this short story collection